I'm Sorry,
Almira Ann

Other Scholastic books for you to enjoy:

A Fairy Called Hilary
By Linda Leopold Strauss

Haunted Summer
By Betty Ren Wright

Lizard Meets Ivana the Terrible
By C. Anne Scott

The Seventh Princess
By Nick Sullivan

Show and Tell
By Stephanie Green

Starting School
By Joanna Hurwitz

Weird Stories from the Lonesome Café
By Judy Cox

I'm Sorry, Almira Ann

JANE KURTZ

WITH ILLUSTRATIONS BY SUSAN HAVICE

A
LITTLE
APPLE
PAPERBACK

SCHOLASTIC INC.

New York Toronto London Auckland Sydney
Mexico City New Delhi Hong Kong Buenos Aires

For my resourceful Grandma Kurtz
and all the rest of my Oregon family—
with thanks to my ancestors
who traveled west on the Oregon Trail

No part of this publication may be reproduced in whole or in part, or stored in a retrieval system, or transmitted in any form or by any means, electronic, mechanical, photocopying, recording, or otherwise, without written permission of the publisher. For information regarding permission, write to Henry Holt and Company, LLC, 115 West 18th Street, New York, NY 10011.

ISBN 0-439-20645-6

Text copyright © 1999 by Jane Kurtz. Illustrations copyright © 1999 by Susan Havice All rights reserved. Published by Scholastic Inc., 555 Broadway, New York, NY 10012, by arrangement with Henry Holt and Company, LLC. SCHOLASTIC, LITTLE APPLE PAPERBACKS, and associated logos are trademarks and/or registered trademarks of Scholastic Inc.

12 11 10 9 8 7 6 5 4 3 2   3 4 5 6/0

Printed in the U.S.A.   40

First Scholastic printing December 2001

CONTENTS

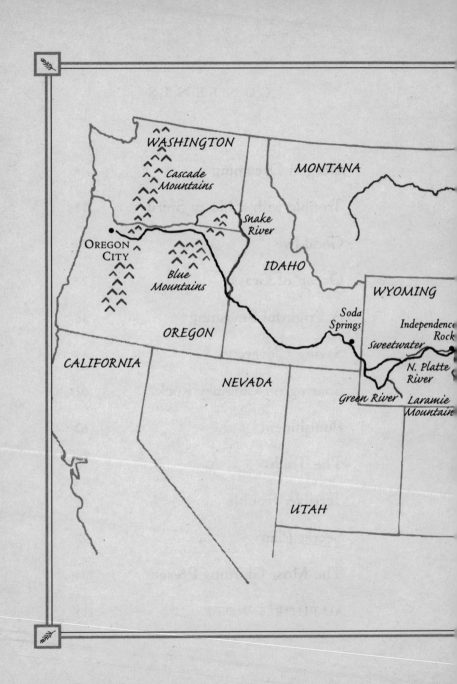

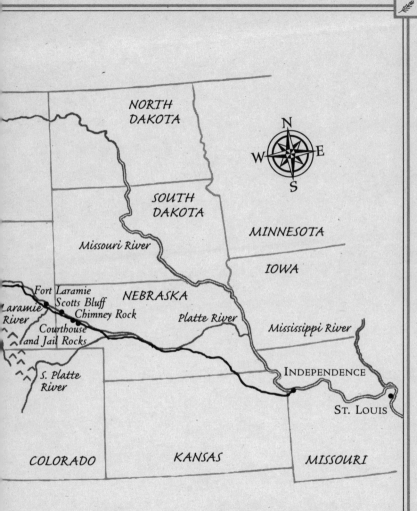

NORTH
DAKOTA

SOUTH
DAKOTA

MINNESOTA

IOWA

Missouri River

NEBRASKA

Fort Laramie
Scotts Bluff
Laramie   Chimney Rock
River   Platte River

Mississippi River

Courthouse
and Jail Rocks

S. Platte
River   INDEPENDENCE

                              ST. LOUIS

COLORADO   KANSAS   MISSOURI

The Oregon Trail

I'm Sorry,
Almira Ann

Oregon Dreaming

Sarah rubbed a cool, smooth egg on her cheek and wondered what it would be like to be inside an egg. Cozy dark? Scary dark? Or would some light come seeping through the eggshell? The most important thing was that she would still be going to Oregon—even if she had to get there inside an egg.

"Have you gone to sleep at your work?" Grandmother asked. Sometimes Grandmother's voice was like a pin, popping the best daydreams.

Sarah stuck the egg deep into the cornmeal. "I was wondering what it would be like to be inside an egg," she said to Almira Ann.

"Yellow," Almira Ann said.

They both giggled.

"Careful," Grandmother said sharply. "You'll poke and giggle and have those eggs all broke before the trip even starts."

"I think it would be nice to be inside an egg," Almira Ann said. "We could ride snug in a bed of cornmeal, all safe, the whole way to Oregon."

Yes, Sarah thought. Unless you bumped against another egg or something. But you wouldn't see very much inside a barrel of cornmeal. She was glad she was riding on the outside.

"Grandma Hastings says we should never go," Almira Ann whispered. "She says she might as well be throwing us like a rock into the vasty deep."

"But you have to go," Sarah said quickly. She bit the tip of her tongue to keep any other words inside. After all, *her* grandmother was going. It was Almira Ann's grandmother who was staying behind in Missouri.

Almira Ann leaned forward. Her blue eyes looked big and worried. "Queen Victoria was scared when she heard Grandma Hastings talk about the vasty deep." Queen Victoria was Almira Ann's doll, who had come all the way from relatives in England. She had a stiff but beautiful face. Grandma Hastings and Almira Ann had worked together for hours and hours to make Queen Victoria's clothes. Today Queen Victoria was wearing a bonnet with little pink roses on the side.

Sarah stuck another egg into the cornmeal and thought about what it would be like if she had to leave her grandmother. Not as bad as if she had to leave Almira Ann. She and Almira Ann had been born eight years ago on the exact same day—July 4. Mama often told the story about how Grandmother had helped born both of them and wrapped them in one of her big quilts.

The Hastings farm was the only nearby farm where another girl lived. So she and Almira Ann had grown up playing together almost every day. And every year, when America celebrated its birthday, she and Almira Ann got to celebrate theirs, too. If she ever had to leave Almira Ann, it would be like an egg white heaving itself up and leaving its shell.

Six-year-old Chatworth burst out the door. A rock, tied to a string, bounced behind him. "Papa said he was almost ready for the eggs. Then he sudden went off. Where's the sugar, anyway?"

"Such noise and commotion," Grandmother huffed. Sometimes Grandmother's voice was like thunderclouds coming up just when Sarah had hung the last heavy quilt on the line. "The sugar is in the kitchen, Chatworth. Must everything sound like the roar of an overgrown river before we even begin this trip?"

"Sorry." Chatworth trotted over to the clothesline and picked up two cones of sugar wrapped in their blue paper. "I want to get started. Where did Papa go? What if everyone gets all the Oregon land before we get there?"

"Mercy!" was all Grandmother said.

Almira Ann put down the egg she was holding. "My mother is probably looking for me," she said to Sarah. She scooped up Queen Victoria and started off as she talked. "She and your mama were talking about how to pack their saleratus to make the cakes and bread rise. By now she might be wonder-worrying where I am."

Almira Ann stopped for a minute to make the doll's hand give a little good-bye wave. Sarah stared after her friend. "Wait," she called. Then she scrambled to her feet and ran after.

As she dashed away, she could hear Grandmother calling, "Sarah . . . this is not . . . ," but she ran so fast the words were gone in no time. She was like a bird with wind whisking her along when she ran this way.

There! She grabbed Almira Ann's hand.

"Mercy!" Almira Ann said in Grandmother's voice. When they had stopped laughing, Almira Ann asked, "Aren't you scared to run out on your grandma like that?"

"Yes," Sarah said, ducking her head. "I shouldn't have done it." She swung both of their hands. Almira Ann's hand was as brown as one of the eggs but not nearly so smooth. Her fingers were thin and delicate. That must be why Almira Ann was such a wonder with a needle and thread.

Almira Ann gave Sarah's fingers a squeeze. "Well, come home with me. You can help me with my packing now."

Sarah stopped. "No," she said slowly. "Mama will be upset if she sees me." A picture of Mama floated into Sarah's head. Mama's hands reaching out to pick up a bird's nest that the wind had flung to the ground. Mama singing as she churned the butter in the cool evening. But if Mama was upset, she could tremble for hours.

At the fork, Sarah let go of Almira Ann's hand and turned off the path. She started to climb the hill, looking back only once to wave.

The rocks were rough on this side, and sometimes she skinned her knees as she climbed up and over. She'd heard people say it was the rocks that made the farm stingy—not giving good crops the way some farms here in Missouri did.

Sarah sighed. She had a bad habit of hiding in corners. People talked when they didn't know she was there. Other people said it wasn't that the land was stingy. It was that Papa was too . . . something. Too ready to drop the plow and climb a mountain and stare up at the way leaves wiggled in the wind. Too dreamy. Those same people would probably have mean words to say about her if they could see her climb like this.

"Why not go on the path?" That's what Grandmother would say. But the path was always the same, and the rocks were different every time. Suddenly her foot slipped. She gasped, then groped until her foot found a better place.

Finally she was safe in the sweet new grass. She turned and turned in the sun, feeling the grass swish against her legs. Wait! Over beyond the blackberry bushes, what was that sound? Something was moving. Something big. Sarah stopped still and listened. She put her hand on her mouth to hush the sound of her panting.

For a second, she thought it was gone. No. Just the pounding in her ears had got so loud. The something was still coming toward her with heavy footsteps.

Trouble with a Hasty Spirit

Sarah felt the whole middle part of her yank itself into a big knot. Where could she hide? Over by that hollow log? No, it wasn't big enough for her to get inside. But it could make a powerful loud noise.

She grabbed up a stick. Papa always said most animals were more scared of you than you were of them. *Wham!* She hit the log as hard as she could. *Wham, wham, wham!*

The footsteps stopped.

"That's right," Sarah yelled. The loud sound of her voice almost made her jump. "Go on back the way you came."

"Sarah?"

Sarah took a step backward. "Who's there?"

Papa started to laugh in his deep, rumbling way. He was still laughing when she poked the blackberry bushes apart with the stick. "Papa, what are you doing up here?" What did he mean, scaring her? "You're supposed to be packing."

"You're supposed to be packing, too."

Sarah felt a smile making the sides of her mouth itch. She ran around the bushes and leaped into Papa's arms.

"Careful," Papa said. "I've got my gun."

His gun. Yes, Sarah thought as they started to walk down the mountain. He could always tell Grandmother he had been trying to get some meat for the trip.

"I was packing, and I missed the top of my mountain," Papa said in a sad, gentle singsong. "I had to come up here where I could see everything."

He stopped and pointed. "Look."

Sarah looked out at the trees that were just

starting to get tiny green leaves. At her house and Almira Ann's house, smoke curled softly out the chimneys.

"My papa brought us here when I was just a baby," Papa said. His voice was full of wonderment. "I guess he thought his family would take root here and be part of this land. Your grandmother never says, but I worry what she thinks about our leaving."

Sarah grabbed Papa's hand. "But we're a moving-on family." Great-grandma and Great-grandpa Benton had been pioneers to Ohio. Grandma and Grandpa Benton had been pioneers to Missouri. Now her own mama and papa had Oregon fever.

But what did Grandmother think? Grandmother's husband had brought her to this place when she was a young woman with little babies and big hopes. No wonder all the edges of her were extra rough and bumpy these days.

"Papa," Sarah said in a small voice. "I ran away from Grandmother again."

Papa's hand around hers felt as tight and heavy as a mudpack. But he said only, "You must say you're sorry as soon as you get home."

Sarah pulled her hand away. "I'm sorry. I'm sorry. It seems like every day of packing, I have to say I'm sorry. I hate it."

Papa tapped the top of her head. "If we didn't have Grandmother watching over the packing, I very much doubt we'd ever be on our way to Oregon."

Sarah sighed. All the rest of the way down the mountain, she could feel herself pulling back, walking more and more slowly. She knew exactly what Grandmother would say in her most scolding tone—"You must tame your hasty spirit, child."

That's what Grandmother had said just last week when Sarah was running too fast and tipped over the butter churn by mistake. A few weeks ago, it was what she said when Sarah snarled her sewing into a huge knot. And Sarah didn't even want to think about the scolding last month when she forgot to latch the goat pen, and the goats got out and chewed on the sheets that Grandmother had just worked on so hard, using dye to turn them a nice, practical brown for the trip.

Sarah said the words to herself in a whiny, squealy whisper. "You must tame your hasty spirit, child." Grandmother would never, never use that voice. Even thinking about Grandmother and that voice made her giggle.

Papa glanced at her. "Look," Sarah said quickly. "I see Mama on the path down there. That's her gingham dress."

Papa didn't say anything. But he started to walk faster.

They caught up with Mama just before they got to the house. Sarah watched Papa twirl Mama around, just as if it were time for doing a little dancing, not a time for packing.

Mama laughed. Then she suddenly pulled away and put her arms behind her back. "Such a day," she said. "My strawberries have dried into bright, red jewels. I should be happy. But when I saw them, I went all deep-down sad, thinking of never weeding those strawberry plants again."

Sarah thought about weeding. Weeding was a

sore back. Weeding was a hot neck. Weeding was stubborn little roots hanging on as tight as they could among all the snaky threads of the strawberry plants. She wouldn't miss that job!

She was about to say so, but Papa gave her a look, and she remembered the scolding she had ahead.

"Papa!" It was Chatworth, calling from over by the wagon. "Papa, come see what I've done with the sugar."

Well, Papa had run off, too, Sarah thought. The unfairness felt like a rock in her throat. Why should she have to say she was sorry when he didn't?

Better get it over with. She turned slowly to the house. Now that they were really and truly getting close to leaving Missouri forever, maybe Grandmother would be too sad to give her much of a scolding.

No, Sarah thought, Grandmother might be sad, but she had her spirit too much under control to show it. As for Sarah's own spirit, she could feel it flapping like a sheet inside her as she opened the door.

Good-bye

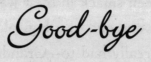

As it turned out, Grandmother said something much worse than "You must tame your hasty spirit, child." She caught Sarah with one of her sharp-as-pins looks. Then she said, "I do not believe we will be going to Oregon after all, Sarah Eliza Benton."

Sarah gasped.

"Certainly," Grandmother went on, "we will never manage a four-month trip of two thousand miles unless someone in this family will get hold of the other end of the log and lift."

Sarah looked at the floor, wondering what Grandmother meant. She knew when Grandfather and Grandmother moved to this farm, lots of logs had been smack in their way. And if anyone could lift one end of a big, old, heavy log—if she really, really had to—Grandmother would be the one.

"I will," Sarah said. "I'll help you lift, Grandmother."

Grandmother sniffed. She poked at the yarn she was untangling. "You!" she said. "I can't think of anyone less reliable. And I will be hugely surprised if this family can get itself on the road."

Sarah fretted about those words every time Grandmother was cross in those April weeks. It was hard to get packed. Papa would pick up his fiddle and forget where he was and start playing a tapping tune.

Mama would come into the house and hear the music. Sometimes she'd laugh and do a little two-step. But you never knew. The music could also make her start to cry. When Papa asked her what was wrong, she would say something like how could she ever leave the laying hens? Grandmother was like a hen herself, pulling and pushing them all into place, running after them every time they forgot.

Sometimes Sarah wondered if they would truly get on the road. She thought about Grandmother's words while they packed the bacon and coffee and beans and salt and vinegar and pickles and dried apples—and put the butter in the middle of the sack of flour. She thought about those words while her family sold the horses and spinning wheels and plow and pitchforks and the sixty-gallon soap kettle.

She thought about Grandmother's words when she listened as Papa stood talking to Almira Ann's pa about the best way to start the trip. It was important not to start off too soon, Almira Ann's pa said, or the cattle, goats, and oxen wouldn't find enough grass to eat. But if they left too late, blizzards could catch them on the other end. Sarah shook her head. So much to plan for. Would Papa be able to plan for everything?

"The guidebooks say no useless trumpery

should be taken," Grandmother reminded everyone several times. She said it for about the fifth time on the day before leaving day.

"I've given most of my fancy things to be traded or sold," Mama said cheerfully. She rubbed her wedding ring. "This is the only trumpery I need. And an old hand mirror in case we want to see what we look like on the way to Oregon." She went back to packing her dearest things—her bandages and liniments and the cuttings from her healing herb plants. Sarah watched as Mama put other things in the medicine bag, whispering their names to make sure she had everything. Butterfly weed and sweet flag root tonics. Ointments of pennyroyal, horsemint, and smartweed.

While Mama worked on her supplies, Papa and Grandmother walked around the room, looking at everything that was left. Grandmother said she didn't need anything like a ring or a mirror. The one thing she wanted—which some, she admitted, might consider trumpery—was the oak dining table with the claw feet. "It made it across the Alleghenies to Ohio," she said. "And then it made the trip to Missouri. I'm sure it can handle a trip to Oregon."

Papa said he would figure out how to fit the table in. "Don't worry," he told Grandmother. "Something will come to me while I tinker with the ropes. I need to think out the best way to tie Clovercup to one of the wagons." For now, they would use their two old farm wagons. It would only take four days to get to Independence and then they would get a big new wagon for the trip.

Sarah watched everybody with a strange, floating feeling in her stomach. Would they really leave? She felt as if she had been holding her breath for months.

Even the next morning, she could hardly believe it was really happening. Chatworth was whooping and racing in circles. Almira Ann's grandmother was crying and kissing everyone. Almira Ann's mother was telling Mama about packing

seven pairs of shoes. "It wouldn't surprise me," she said, "if my first pair were already worn out by the time we reach Independence."

Mama looked down at her own feet with a worried glance. For a moment, Sarah was afraid she would insist they couldn't leave after all. Not until she had another pair of shoes made for everyone.

Papa cracked the whip at the oxen. "Chatworth," he called. "You're in charge of the goats until we meet up with other folks in Independence. Do your best to keep them moving along."

Amazing, Sarah thought as the wagon wheels began to creak. They were on their way. She waved good-bye to the house, full of a sparkling joy.

For the first mile or two, she felt as strong as the oxen that were pulling the wagon. Papa said after Independence, when they bought the big wagon, she could ride inside when she got tired. But she was never going to get tired. Almira Ann trudged beside her, wrapped in one of Grandmother Hastings's old shawls, hugging Queen Victoria, who was wearing her best green silk dress.

Sarah put her arm around her friend. Almira Ann let out a huge sniffle. Poor Almira Ann. Her mother didn't want to go. Her grandmother had refused to go. But Almira Ann's father had said, "People are settling right under our noses here. We'd be fools not to go to Oregon, where the rivers are full of fish and one huge tree can give enough lumber for a whole house." Sarah could hardly wait to see a tree like that—a tree that Papa said seven men couldn't reach all the way around.

"Do you think we'll be lost in the vasty deep?" Almira Ann asked.

"I'm sure we won't. Don't worry," Sarah said. But she herself felt a little worried. Was her family the type to make it all the way to Oregon? Could all the people and the goats and Clovercup and the oxen walk two thousand miles? And what would they do if they ran into logs that no one was strong enough to lift?

Ocean of Grass

By the middle of the morning, Sarah had to admit that she *was* going to get tired after all. She was walking so slowly that one of the goats came up and tried to nibble on her dress. "Go away!" Almira Ann said, stomping her foot at the goat. Almira Ann sounded tired, too.

"Maybe we should get up and ride for a little while," Sarah said. "Look." Papa was lifting Chatworth onto one of the farm wagons to take a rest. The oxen were poking along, so she and Almira Ann could probably climb onto the wagon without any help. But Papa had said they must never climb up or jump down from a moving wagon.

"I don't know." Almira Ann gave the wagon an uneasy glance. "Maybe when we get the big wagons, I wouldn't mind riding."

"I wish that wagon had a feather bed on it," Sarah said. "I'd lie down and sleep all the way to Independence."

Mama walked by and gave Sarah a smile. "We'll be nooning soon," she said. "If you want, you can ride this afternoon."

Sarah thought she might have to lie down by the side of the road. But Almira Ann wasn't complaining. So Sarah bit her tongue and kept going, too.

When they finally stopped, she thought she had never felt anything so delicious as the shade of the tree where they sat and ate the homemade rolls and cheese Grandma Hastings had sent along. "This afternoon will be easy," she told Almira Ann. "We'll be riding."

But riding turned out to be hard, too. The wagon bounced and jostled until her teeth rattled. Sarah stared down at a goat that was pulling a mouthful of grass from beside the road. Chatworth whacked its leg with a stick to get it back with the others. Up ahead, Mama was talking to Grandmother and Almira Ann's mother. Was Mama limping a little? They had three more days before they got to Independence. What if they couldn't even get that far?

Sarah didn't feel as if she could let out her breath until they were all the way through Independence and had traveled for two days out on the prairie. They hadn't found any logs in the road yet. They had gotten off by May 10th. And they were really and truly on the way to Oregon.

Sarah let out a huge, whistling sigh. She looked around. Nothing but grass. The way it rippled when the wind whooshed across it made her want to laugh and hop and whirl. It would be easy to get lost in this ocean of grass, though. She had to be sure not to let the wagons out of her sight.

Thirteen other wagons had joined up with them in Independence. The first night, all the men voted on some rules and chose a man named Abraham Foss to be captain. Sometimes Captain Foss let the fifteen wagons spread out across the prairie until they looked like one giant wave going forward, but right now they were in a line, each one following the next. Thanks to Papa, Sarah could instantly pick out her own new wagon. Papa had found a way to make it the most cheerful wagon in the line—the cover was red!

They had already walked through places where it would be easy to get lost. Where the grass was higher than Papa, even. The captain had to stand on top of his wagon to see over the waving grasses and help them find their way.

But here, the grass was shorter. It looked like a vast green carpet filled with thousands of tiny yellow flowers, too beautiful for words. The minute Mama saw the flowers, she had begun to fill her apron with them. And the goats were eating their fill. Too bad Clovercup couldn't find some way to untie herself from behind the wagon.

Sarah could just imagine it. The cow was untying her rope. She was trotting away from the wagons. Then, with a huge leap, she was diving into the grass, rolling all around, tearing off huge mouthfuls. Sarah giggled.

"What's so funny?"

Sarah whirled. "Oh, Almira Ann. Isn't it glorious?"

Almira Ann looked a little pale. Ever since Independence, her papa had made her ride in the wagon. And the new wagons turned out to be just as bumpity as the old ones. "I'm glad you came to walk with me," Sarah said. "I've missed you."

Almira Ann leaned over to pick some yellow flowers. "Pa didn't want me to. Look at how those dark clouds are boiling up over there. He says bad weather could soon be upon us. But I begged and begged."

Sarah stared at the clouds. They *were* dark and mean looking. How far away were they? How long would it take to run back to the wagons?

"Hey!"

Sarah turned around. It was only Chatworth and a friend. Now that there were other boys, Chatworth didn't always have to be watching the goats.

The boys ran up, panting. "Did you see the storm coming?" Chatworth asked.

"The older boys say storms in Kansas Territory can split the whole earth in two," his friend shouted. "They say we're in for a wicked smashing," he added before dashing off.

Almira Ann gasped.

"Just hush up!" Sarah said. She waved her hand in a big arc. "Aren't you glad we're finally out here in Kansas Territory?" she asked Almira Ann.

"Not me," Chatworth said. "Independence was grand. The best place I ever saw."

Sarah shook her head. "Too many people. *Right* under our noses."

"Too much banging and clanging," Almira Ann said. "Too much hammering and shouting."

"Well, anyway," Sarah said, "we got our wagons and all. And they're wonderful."

"They're wonderful!" Chatworth shouted.

"And when we get to Oregon, Papa says there will be fat pigs already cooked, running around with knives and forks in them."

Almira Ann didn't say anything. She had started to weave the yellow flowers into a tiny halo as they walked. Probably she was planning to take it back for Queen Victoria.

Sarah picked some yellow flowers and tried to do the same thing, watching Almira Ann's fingers. "Aren't the wagons the most wonderful thing you ever saw?"

"Well . . ." Almira Ann ducked her head. "Yes. But my pa said your pa was crazy to get a red wagon cover," she added in a low voice. "Everyone knows they're supposed to be white."

Sarah frowned. "I think it's very, very beautiful. And the sailmaker said why not." She didn't like the way her stomach was feeling. She didn't like thinking that Almira Ann should shut her mouth and go back in her own wagon.

Whoomp. A gunshot of thunder cracked across the sky. Somewhere a startled cow let out a bellow. Sarah could hear the captain shouting.

And yes, there was Grandmother's voice. "Sarah! Chatworth!"

The clouds rolled and boiled overhead and the wind pushed at them, yanking on their skirts. "Do you think the earth will really split in two?" Almira Ann shouted above the wind.

"Of course not," Sarah shouted back as they started to run. But her eyes were watering from the wind, and she could feel her heart whamming in her chest like a runaway cow. A storm was one thing when you were in a good, strong log house. What would happen to them in houses that had wheels on the bottom and canvas on the top? All kinds of strange things could happen in the middle of this ocean of grass that seemed to have no beginning and no end.

A Frightful Smashing

They'd only run a few yards when Sarah felt the first cold raindrop against her forehead. A bright flash of lightning forked across the sky. Chatworth let out a howl. "Don't stop running," Sarah yelled above the thunder. With a roar, the rain whooshed over them.

Sarah could barely make out the milling wagons. She knew the drivers must be shouting and cracking their whips, trying to move the oxen, trying to get the wagons into a circle. But she couldn't hear anything over the roar of the rain—not even the squishing sound of her shoes, as full of water as if she'd been wading in a stream.

They reached her wagon first. The oxen were standing in place and, at the back, Papa was fumbling with Clovercup's rope, his beard streaming with water. "Papa," Sarah hollered as loud as she could holler. "Need help?"

He gave a wild wave of his arm. She thought she heard something about "get inside" and "tangled." Almira Ann helped her push and heave Chatworth into the wagon. Almira Ann went next. Sarah scrambled up last, slipping and sliding on the wet wood.

Inside, Mama reached out her arms. The pale flicker of the lightning made everything pink. Mama's dark eyes looked like big, shiny buttons in her light pink face. Chatworth burst into tears and crawled over to her. Sarah barely heard the murmuring sound of Mama's voice, soothing Chatworth, as Grandmother flung a quilt over the girls' heads.

For a moment, holding hands under the quilt

with Almira Ann, Sarah felt safe and snug. Then a crack of thunder split the air, sounding as if it would crash the top of the wagon down on them all. Almira Ann screamed.

Sarah stuck her head out from the side of the quilt. "Stop that thunderous noise," she yelled, shaking her fist at the sky. "Stop it right now."

Almira Ann started to laugh. Another clap of thunder made the wagon tremble. Outside, Sarah could see rain spraying up as it hit the ground.

Almira Ann reached over and hugged Sarah. "You're so brave," she said. Then she whispered, "And my pa was wrong. I think your wagon is just beautiful."

Suddenly it was all over. The thunder faded to a grumbling sound. A last flicker of lightning made the canvas glow pink again for a second. The rain stopped roaring and became a thumping sound and then the flick-flicking of drizzle on the roof.

Almira Ann pushed the quilt away from her head. Her braids were coming undone, and she looked like a wet puppy. "That was dreadful!"

she said. "I need to get to my wagon. I need to make sure Mama and Papa and Queen Victoria are all right."

Sarah helped her out and listened to the squishing sound of Almira Ann's shoes as she ran off through the puddles. She could hear lots of sounds now. But something . . . something wasn't right.

Sarah scrambled out of the wagon, pushing the wet dress impatiently away as it grabbed at her legs, trying to trip her as she slid down. Sure enough, just as she had thought. No mooing sound from the back of the wagon. No Clover-cup. Papa stood in a daze, water dripping from his beard, staring at the rope in his hand.

"Papa!" Sarah rushed toward him, not worrying about the mud that splashed up.

"I was trying to untangle the rope."

He looked awful, Sarah thought, scared and helpless.

"That last thundering . . . well . . . suddenly I couldn't hold her anymore. She jerked her head back and . . ."

"Why did you untie the rope, Papa?" As soon as she said the words, Sarah wished she could yank them back. No need to make Papa feel worse than he already did. "Come on," she said, grabbing out for his hand. "Almira Ann's pa will help. We'll find her. I'm sure we will."

Sarah thought she had never felt worse, trudging around a muddy prairie in a drizzling rain, looking for a cow. "Clovercup," she called. She stopped and listened. All she heard was Chatworth's echo. "Clooooovercup."

She shook the rain out of her eyes and tried to imagine where she would go if she were a cow. She could almost see Clovercup's big eyes, dark as melting chocolate, staring out from the rain. Poor Clovercup. What must she think to be pulled out of her nice, safe barn and prodded down the road, then herded through the noisy streets of Independence, and now lost in an ocean of prairie mud?

A shape lurched out of the grass, startling

her. Chatworth. "Papa says they found her," he panted. "Papa says she's in a bad spot. Papa says we're to go back to the wagon so he doesn't have to worry about us, too."

Sarah stamped. Mud splattered everywhere, and Chatworth jumped back with a yelp. She wanted to see Clovercup for herself. And what did it mean—a bad spot? But it wouldn't do to disobey Papa. "Tell me everything," she said as they started walking back.

Clovercup had somehow slid into a ravine, Chatworth said. They would have to think of a way to get her out. It might not be possible in this rain, though. Papa said they couldn't even see for sure if she was hurt.

Sarah couldn't tell if she was crying or if that was just rain on her face. She certainly felt like crying. Poor, poor Clovercup.

They trudged up to the wagon. Grandmother was standing outside. As Sarah got closer, she saw that Grandmother was holding an umbrella over herself and the fire. "I heard," Grandmother said as soon as she saw Sarah. "Well,

what can be done with a cow that gets a hasty spirit in her and runs off?"

Sarah sniffled.

"Well!" Grandmother said again. "Fretting won't make anything better. Here—you'll feel cheered just as soon as this bread gets done." She bent over, and Sarah heard raindrops from the umbrella sizzle as they hit the black pot. "Hot bread," Grandmother said. "A slice of hot bread and butter will pull most people's wits back into place."

Sarah leaned against the wagon, shivering. Hot bread would be good. And it smelled as if Mama was brewing up a pot of ginger tea. But what about Clovercup? Would she really stay put? Sarah tried to think what would help Clovercup get her wits back in place so she could somehow get out of the ravine.

Saving Clovercup

When Papa came dragging back to camp, saying that it was getting too dark to do anything for Clovercup, Sarah thought she would never sleep. And she stayed awake for a very long time in the tent, shivering under the damp quilt. After she finally did drift off, she woke up often, imagining that she could hear Clovercup mooing somewhere in the distance.

Once, when she found herself lying as stiff as a stick and wide awake under the quilt, she crawled to the mouth of the tent and looked out. The clouds had all washed away, and the sky was a fright of blazing stars. "Sleep well, Clovercup,"

Sarah whispered. The smell of the campfire hung in the air, and she imagined a trickle of smoke carrying her words off to tickle the cow's ears.

The minute she heard Papa stirring the next morning, she hurried out to walk with him to where the ravine was like a black mouth opening in the prairie. Papa climbed into the ravine while Sarah stared down anxiously. After a little while, Papa climbed back out. Clovercup was fine, he said. But the sides of the ravine were slick with yesterday's rain. He couldn't find a way to get her out.

After a while, Almira Ann came to stare down into the ravine with Sarah. Some men from the camp clumped together nearby, talking about what could be done. "You were awfully brave in the storm yesterday," Almira Ann said. "I thought the world really was splitting in two."

Almira Ann's eyes glowed with admiration. Sarah blushed. She felt warm even in her damp dress and shoes.

Suddenly there was Papa. His face looked grave. "No one can think of any way to get Clovercup out," he said. "It's exceeding sad, I know, but the captain says we might have to leave her."

Sarah's hands leaped to her face, as if his words had rushed out and slammed into her. She sat down with a thump. "No, Papa," she said. "If Clovercup doesn't go on, I won't, either."

For a few minutes, nobody said anything. Then Papa gave a great sigh and turned to walk back to the camp. Almira Ann touched Sarah's arm. "Let me see what my pa says," she said. "Maybe he will have an idea by now."

When they were gone, Sarah sat like a cold lump of butter for what felt like a long, long time. The prairie felt huge and lonely around her. How would she survive if they really left her? She shivered. Mama and Papa would never do that. Would they?

She looked around. Not a tree or bush in sight. Out on the Great Plains, nothing even existed to build a house. Grandmother surely didn't have to worry about logs in the road here. It was a good thing Oregon had those giant trees. Otherwise they might never have a house again.

After a while, Sarah could hear a buzzing of voices, but she didn't look up. They were probably going to try to move her. She glanced around for a root or something she could hang on to. "I won't go," she called into the ravine. "I vow to you, Clovercup, and I always keep my vows."

"Sarah!" It was Almira Ann's voice. "Sarah, your papa has an idea. They're going to try it."

"They're going to try it!" Chatworth yelled behind her. "They're going to try it!"

When Sarah heard the plan, her knotted stomach began to buzz as if she'd swallowed a hive of bees. The plan sounded terrible. They were going to bore holes in Clovercup's horns and see if they could pull her up the steep side. Was this just a crazy Papa idea? "I can't watch," Sarah wailed.

"I'll watch," Chatworth said.

"Come on," Almira Ann said to Sarah. "Let's go back to the wagons. We don't want to hear poor Clovercup mooing and bawling, do we?"

"It's all right," Chatworth called after them. "Mama is going to go down into the ravine to sing 'Oh, Susanna' to Clovercup to make her brave."

Sarah felt sick as they walked back. But Almira Ann told her that she just needed breakfast. And Grandmother said that idle hands made a worrisome mind, so Sarah should wash up yesterday's dirty tin plates.

Before long, Chatworth came dashing back to the wagon, screaming, "It worked! It worked!" Mama ran close behind him.

"My land!" Grandmother said. "We're lucky Clovercup is a sturdy old girl with a very strong spirit."

Mama and Chatworth danced around, holding hands and laughing. Almira Ann lifted the last plate out of the water and shook it. Water drops gleamed in the bright prairie air. Almira Ann's eyes gleamed, too. "It never would have happened except for you," she said to Sarah. "They were just going to give up. You saved Clovercup by not letting them leave her behind."

Sarah felt relief flood through her down to

her bones. Clovercup was saved. Neither she nor Clovercup would have to stay forever on the prairie. And the look in Almira Ann's eyes made her stomach as warm as the dishwater around her hands.

Soaring on Chimney Rock

That warm feeling stayed with her as the trip dragged on, day after tiring day. Every morning, they had to be up by six to take down the tents and load the wagons. By seven, when the captain's horn called out, whips started cracking and the yokes groaned as the oxen started to move. They usually traveled for twenty miles every day. Twenty long miles. Each night, Pa read a chapter from *Pilgrim's Progress*. Sarah thought she knew just how poor Pilgrim felt on his endless journey.

Sarah tried to think whether anyone she knew had ever traveled more than two or three days at a time. Her hair itched under her sunbonnet. If only she could take the sunbonnet off. But Grandmother would say, "You'll soon be as speckled as a turkey egg." Sarah didn't dare.

When the captain said they were about two hundred miles past Independence, they came to the Platte River. Papa laughed at the river and said it was flowing bottom side up. "It's too dirty to wash clothes in and too thick to drink," Grandmother complained. Sarah still saw no trees. Only pale cliffs far off to the side of the river.

For a long time, they followed the same path as the Platte. When they'd been on the road for about a month, they had to cross the south fork of the river. All the men worked together to take the wheels off the wagons so they could be floated over like boats. After that, the trail became one adventure after another, up hills and down steep drops on the other side. At night, they gathered buffalo chips because there was no wood to build their fires. The first time Sarah was sent to gather some she wrinkled her nose in disgust. But soon she and Chatworth thought nothing of sailing the dried droppings across the prairie.

Finally one day, the captain said they had left the Great Plains and were on the High Plains. Sarah felt as if they'd been out here on the prairie forever. The carpet of flowers had slowly disappeared. Now all they saw was tough buffalo grass and hard, dusty ground.

She was tired of the goats that always seemed to be chewing on everything people left lying around the camp. She was tired of milking Clovercup out in the dust. Sometimes she found herself thinking hateful thoughts, almost wishing the cow had stayed stuck in the bottom of the ravine. She even tried trading jobs with Chatworth. She would grease the wheels from the tar bucket to help keep them from drying and cracking. But Chatworth said no.

Early in June, Papa pointed to the horizon, and when Sarah squinted, she could make out a line of mountains. "The Laramie Mountains," Papa said. "They're a sign that we're headed toward the Rockies." During the next few weeks, he pointed to other famous sights of the trail—Jail Rock, Courthouse Rock, and finally the faint outline of Chimney Rock, jutting out like a tall, sharp finger.

In the clear air, Chimney Rock seemed to be only a little ways off. But before long, Sarah began to feel she had stared at Chimney Rock for days and it had gotten no closer.

By now, it was the middle of June, and everyone seemed tired of the trip except for Mama. Mama usually walked with the other women ahead of the wagons, a laughing, merry group. While the flowers lasted, she collected them and dried them. She found other treasures in the prairie grass, too, like wild strawberries, red and tart. When the flowers ran out, she seemed still to be able to find treasures—a sparkling stone or a tall shoot with a yucca blossom at the top.

During the campfires at night, Mama loved to sing to the fiddle songs. One moonlit night, she coaxed Grandmother and Almira Ann's mother to help and they all made molasses candy. In the daytime, she often went to wagons where people were sick, taking her tonics and her ointments and her teas. Mama's feet got more and more sore until she finally walked barefoot, but she didn't complain.

"Does your mama still have seven pairs of shoes?" Sarah asked when they were riding in Almira Ann's wagon one day. Almira Ann was making a delicate lace fan for Queen Victoria.

"No," Almira Ann said. "She has to keep throwing pairs away."

Sarah wished Mama had more shoes to throw away. She also wished she had Almira Ann's fingers instead of her own clumsy ones. She would never be able to make something like the lace fan.

"Look," Almira Ann said. "Let me show you all the things I've made for Queen Victoria."

Sarah watched as Almira Ann pulled things out of the bag. Queen Victoria now had a flounce to put on the bottom of her dress. She had a cape, decorated with pearls, and a velvet muff. She had bonnets with rosebuds and ribbons. For fancy, she had a satin hat with a tiny feather Almira Ann had found on the prairie.

Sarah felt an ugly feeling stirring inside. Envy. That was the name of the feeling. Grandmother said envy would eat away at your spirit and rob you of happiness and everything dear. It was true. Sarah didn't feel happy. "You know," she said, "it isn't very patriotic playing with a doll named Queen Victoria when it's this close to America's birthday."

Almira Ann looked up in surprise. "We're not even in America anymore. And you know my grandmother in England sent her to me. She said the real Queen Victoria is young but stately, just like my doll."

"All the more reason to be patriotic," Sarah said. "Anyway, Papa says he's sure one day our flag will have two more stars. One for Oregon. One for California."

Almira Ann studied Sarah's face. "Would you like to hold Queen Victoria for a while?" she asked.

Sarah blushed. It was almost as if Almira Ann had seen the envy inside her. "No," she said quickly.

After a minute, Almira Ann looked down. Then she said, "I made something to give you. I was going to save it for our birthday."

Almira Ann reached down into the bag and pulled out a rag doll. "Now we both have dolls," she said. It had a little satin dress with a red ribbon.

"Thank you very much," Sarah said coldly. She liked the rag doll, but it was nowhere near as glorious as Queen Victoria. Suddenly she couldn't stand to be in this wagon with all Almira Ann's things. "Let's walk," she said.

"We're not supposed to get down when the wagon is moving."

Sarah stared stubbornly at her friend. "I'm getting out." She climbed onto the tongue, balanced a minute, then leaped down. After a few minutes, Almira Ann followed.

"I miss the flowers," Sarah said as they walked beside the wagon.

"I miss having a bed."

"I miss fresh vegetables." Sarah made a face. "Aren't you tired of bread and bacon? And dried apples? Ugh. I'd rather get scurvy." She studied a prairie dog that popped his head out of a hole up ahead. She wished she could catch one of the fuzzy, quick animals. Papa said the prairie dogs had whole towns—with houses and tunnels—underneath the ground. She'd like to see that underground village.

Almira Ann stooped to pull a long stem of grass and tied the lace fan to Queen Victoria's hand. "I miss my grandmother," she said. "I wonder what she's doing right now."

The sadness in Almira Ann's voice made Sarah's stomach curl up. She should never have started the conversation. "I know," she said quickly. "We should take a little cutoff and go see Chimney Rock close up. We walk much faster than the old oxen. See how close it is now?"

Almira Ann turned to look. "All right," she said slowly.

Sarah felt grandly brave as they turned and walked toward the rock. But the walk was much longer than it looked. It seemed about an hour before they really were close, scrambling up the shale at the base of the rock.

"It's so big!" Almira Ann said, staring up. Her voice was tired.

Sarah felt a stab of guilt. And they still had to walk all the way back.

"And look at all the names," Almira Ann added.

Sarah studied the names, craning her neck to see how far they reached. "I'm going to climb up and write our names," she said suddenly. She scooped up a small rock to carve with.

Almira Ann gasped. "Sarah, you mustn't!" But that only made the idea feel all the more important.

The first part of the climb took only about ten minutes, but the closer Sarah got, the more huge and towering Chimney Rock seemed above her. She had never climbed to so giddy a height. She didn't dare look down.

Finally she came to a place so steep that someone had cut footholds in the soft rock. There

must have been a hundred names carved in the rock. If she could just get a little higher. Oh, she wished she could see the look in Almira Ann's eyes now.

Sarah held her breath and began to climb. Up. Up. Someone had cut notches and driven in little sticks. Sarah hesitated. Then, in a whoosh, she felt a wild, fine spirit grab her. If others had gone this high, she would go even higher.

"Sarah!" Almira Ann's shriek finally stopped her. Well, this was high enough. She must be higher than any living thing could go—except birds. Carefully she scratched their names with the rock.

Coming down was harder, and she felt herself shaking. But finally she was there, sliding down the last few feet of rock toward Almira Ann. "I did it!" she said. "We're up there now forever."

But to Sarah's amazement, Almira Ann didn't cheer and clap. She didn't look up at Sarah with glowing eyes of admiration. No, Almira Ann burst into tears.

Punishment

On the long walk back, Sarah tried to talk about how it felt up there—how she could feel the wind wrapping her in its arms. How she knew the way a bird must feel just before it flies. But Almira Ann said, "Just stop talking about it. Every time I imagine you up so high, it makes my stomach hurt all over again."

Sarah stared down at the ground. A mosquito buzzed near her ear, and she swatted at it. "I wanted to give you the best present in the whole world," she muttered.

"Well, you didn't!" Almira Ann said. "You just scared me."

Sarah looked at Almira Ann. Suddenly she was hotter and more tired than she had ever been. She felt angry at everything. At Almira Ann's tiny fingers that could make such beautiful things for Queen Victoria. At Almira Ann's mother's shoes. At Queen Victoria, with her smug, bland face. She started to walk as fast as she could.

"Wait!" Almira Ann called.

Sarah walked even faster. She was almost running. Then she *was* running. She heard Almira Ann's footsteps running after her. Just then, Almira Ann gave a great yelp.

Sarah stopped. She turned around. "You made me run right into a cactus," Almira Ann wailed. "Look. I'll never get Queen Victoria's lace fan out from the thorns. And her silk dress is torn. And I have cactus needles in my fingers."

Good, Sarah thought. She didn't want to be thinking such mean thoughts. But her feelings were all snarled.

They walked the rest of the way without saying a word to each other. When they reached the camp, Sarah discovered more scared people. The captain had made them strike camp early to look for the missing girls. Everyone in the whole camp, it seemed, had been looking for them.

Almira Ann's mother ran up and scooped up Almira Ann, holding her as close as a baby. "How could you run off like that?" she said. "Why, the Indians might have gotten you."

As for Grandmother, Sarah had never seen her so fierce. "Mercy, mercy me!" she said. "I do believe instead of taming that spirit, you are letting it be more wild than it has ever been." Even Mama looked at her sideways and only patted her hand quickly before going off to put the spider skillet on the fire.

That night, Grandmother let Sarah know she was not welcome to join the singing of "Oh, Susanna" and "She'll Be Coming Around the Mountain" at the campfire. And the next morning, Grandmother said Sarah must ride in the wagon all day, since she couldn't be trusted to not run off.

"I can be trusted now," Sarah protested. But Grandmother had already turned away.

"Where's Mama?" Sarah asked Chatworth.

"Helping in one of the wagons. Mrs. Tinker is sick."

Sarah had never been so miserable. No wonder only sick people and little children rode for long in the wagons. Wagons were too stuffed with flour and beans, coffee and vinegar, plows and rocking chairs, three-legged skillets and clocks. Wagons bounced and squeaked.

Her face felt puffy where she touched it and hurt like a toothache. When she stared into Mama's hand mirror, she saw that mosquito bites had made her face swell. By the nooning stop, her cheeks were so swollen, she could hardly see out of her eyes. She whispered to the rag doll, telling it how miserable she was.

That afternoon, she fell asleep and woke to find that her arm, where it had rested against some bare wood, was rubbed raw from the bouncing of the wagon. She was hot. Her face still hurt. She wanted to just howl. So she did.

"Sarah?" It was Chatworth's voice outside the wagon.

"What?" She scrunched to the front and peered out.

"Mama's making a surprise. It's for tonight when we stop."

Sarah still felt like howling. But she was also a bit curious. Mama knew how to make glorious surprises.

When they stopped, she didn't dare show her face. Finally Papa's head appeared in the wagon opening. "Come here," he said gently. Papa patted flour and water on Sarah's face. "I think that will take a bit of the sting away," he said. Sarah stared at her face in Mama's mirror and had to laugh at how she looked.

Mama gave her a forgiving hug, which took a little more of the sting away. "You go invite our old neighbors to join us around the fire," Mama told Chatworth. "I believe Sarah has some amends to make with her friend."

Sarah looked down at her feet, but she couldn't stay looking down for long. What an interesting place—with reddish clay towers like a castle. "It's called Scotts Bluff," Papa said. "After Hiram Scott, a fur trader who died here."

"How did he die?" Sarah asked. But before Papa could answer, there was Chatworth, coming back. And behind him was Almira Ann's pa, Almira Ann's mother, and, best of all, Almira Ann. As they came up to the fire, though, Almira Ann wouldn't even look at Sarah.

"Mama made something wonderful for us," Chatworth whispered to Sarah. Sarah smiled at him. She wondered if Almira Ann would talk to her again. At least Chatworth was being nice.

And Mama's treat was truly glorious. She had made cookies in the shape of animals. Mama was such an artist that you could even tell what the animals were really supposed to be.

"But you must have used up all your sugar!" Almira Ann's mother said.

"A goodly amount of it," Mama admitted. "We only have a little left now, for very special occasions. But this is a special day, too. After all, our dear daughters who were lost are found."

"Anyway, we'll be in Oregon before you know it," Papa said. "I'm sure we'll have lots of sugar there."

"And fat pigs," Chatworth reminded him. "All cooked, with knives and forks already in them."

Sarah felt tears pushing at the corners of her eyes. Almira Ann hadn't said a word to her. She studied her cookie. She would cherish it forever. She would never, ever eat it. Well, maybe just a little mouse nibble because it had been so long since she had had anything sweet. But that was all.

Out of the corner of her eye, Sarah could see that Almira Ann was nibbling just a bit of her cookie, too.

"Do I look as bad as you look?" Sarah whispered.

Almira Ann finally turned. "You look much worse," she said. Sarah was relieved to hear that Almira Ann sounded as if she were trying not to smile.

"Wretched?" Sarah asked. She patted the stiff flour on her face, trying not to think about how it must look.

"Wretched."

Sarah opened her mouth to ask about the cactus prickles. She would try to say she was sorry, too.

"Look!" Chatworth said suddenly. "Indians."

"They must be Sioux," Papa said. "The captain said Sioux hunting parties were likely to be out among the buffalo this time of year."

Sarah's stomach jumped. Riding toward them across the prairie were the brightest, most magnificent people she had ever seen. And Grandmother should talk about her wild spirit? Here were people who looked as if they knew everything there was to know about wild, free spirits.

The Trade

Sarah looked around. The wagons were in their big nighttime circle, with the animals inside. Why were the Sioux riding straight for their wagon? Maybe it was because of the beautiful red cover.

"I've got to get back to our tent," Almira Ann said. Her voice was scared. "I left Queen Victoria all alone." Before Sarah could say a word, she was gone. Almira Ann's mother gave a squeal and grabbed her husband's hand. They hurried away after Almira Ann.

As the Sioux rode up, the captain and some other men came walking from the other direction. This was the most adventuresome thing to happen yet on the Oregon Trail, Sarah thought. She scooped up the rag doll, grabbed Chatworth's hand, and scrambled behind a big wheel of the wagon, waiting to see what would happen.

From behind the wheel, she looked out at the rest of her family. Grandmother had picked up a heavy black frying pan, but she didn't move from where she sat. Grandmother's face looked watchful. Mama looked amazed and delighted. Papa said something to one of the men, and the man got off his horse. He picked up Mama's hand mirror and held it up, studying his face in it. He laughed, and others gathered around. All the tension seemed to suddenly dissolve.

Chatworth scrambled away from Sarah and, within a few minutes, was running in circles, chasing a Sioux boy in a quick game of tag. A girl about Sarah's age watched them. Sarah stared at the exquisite beads the girl wore around her neck. A deep, longing spirit tugged at her. What would it be like to have beads like that?

Papa made some gestures to the man with the mirror. The other man made gestures, too. Papa turned to Mama and said something. Mama laughed and gave a little wave of her hand.

Papa was trading away Mama's mirror. Sarah watched to see what he was going to get for it. A pair of moccasins. Papa bent down and put the moccasins on Mama's feet, just as if he were bringing beautiful shoes to a queen. He also got some buffalo meat, so they'd have something besides bacon to eat tomorrow night.

As Sarah watched, other people began to trade. Suddenly Sarah had a wonderful idea. She crawled out from behind the wagon wheel and walked all the way around the girl, studying her soft deerskin coat decorated with more beads. Then she stood still while the girl walked all the way around her.

The girl reached out her hand toward Sarah's floured face. Sarah pushed the girl's hand away. The girl smiled and said something Sarah didn't understand. Slowly Sarah pointed to the beads.

For a long moment, the girl stared off, as if Sarah wasn't there at all.

Then, so quickly that it made Sarah jump, the girl turned and pointed. She was pointing to the cookie and the rag doll Sarah clutched in one of her hands.

Sarah swallowed. She could almost taste the crumbly sweetness of the cookie Mama had made. And Almira Ann had made the rag doll for her.

But a hot, fierce longing for the beads filled her chest. She wanted those beads more than she had ever wanted anything in her life. And surely Almira Ann wouldn't mind about the doll. In fact, Almira Ann would probably make another doll for Sarah. Almira Ann's fingers were so nimble, they could make another rag doll easily.

Slowly Sarah held out the rag doll and the cookie. The girl loosened her beads. And then the beads were in Sarah's own hand. All around her now people were still trading—flour and beans for buffalo robes and meat. But she had the only thing that was important to her.

When people gathered around the campfire that night to sing and the fiddles were playing, Sarah couldn't stop looking at her beads. She hoped Almira Ann would come to the campfire so she could show her. But Almira Ann was nowhere to be seen.

The next morning, she had to help with chores. "Don't you even think of running off, now," Grandmother warned. "I do not want our wagon to be the last in line, where the oxen near to choke on everyone else's dust." But as soon as everything was ready and Sarah knew the horn would be sounding any minute, she ducked away from Grandmother and raced over to Almira Ann's wagon.

Almira Ann's pa was checking the grease bucket on the back of the wagon.

Sarah climbed onto the tongue and hopped in. Almira Ann was lying under a quilt in a little space on the floor. "Come out," Sarah said, tugging at the quilt. "I have something great to show you."

When Almira Ann saw the beads, the look in her eyes was all Sarah could have hoped for. She carefully ran her finger over them. "Look at the colors," she said in wonderment.

Sarah grinned. She *knew* Almira Ann would think the beads were a treasure. Who cared about a swollen face when her friend wasn't mad at her anymore? She swallowed, trying to decide how to tell Almira Ann about trading away the rag doll. Surely Almira Ann would understand.

Sarah took a deep breath. As she started to explain what had happened, Almira Ann began to frown. "But don't you see . . . ," Sarah said.

"*Arrrrrrrrrr.*" A strange growling interrupted her. It sounded as if it were coming from just outside the wagon.

Almira Ann grabbed Sarah's arm. Sarah tried to look brave. But she thought she was going to choke on her own breath. What was happening?

"*Arrgggggh.*" Something thumped three times on the outside of the wagon.

Almira Ann shrieked and dove under the quilt. "Wait!" Sarah said. "Let me under, too."

The next few moments were hot and silent. Was hiding under a quilt really going to do any good? Sarah tried to remember something that might be nearby in the crowded wagon—something she could grab and swing with. She held her breath, trying to think. Then a hand grabbed her foot.

Sarah screamed. She threw off the quilt. Whatever it was, she was going to fight it.

Chatworth burst into laughter. "Got you," he said, scrambling up into the wagon. "I scared you! I scared you!"

Sarah crossed her arms over her chest. "What a mean trick," she said.

"Well, I could have been a grizzly bear," he said. "The boys say that's most probably what got Hiram Scott. His friends found his skeleton in the bluffs."

"Don't talk such nonsense," Sarah said.

Almira Ann pulled the quilt up to her chin and tucked it around herself and Queen Victoria. The horn sounded. Sarah heard a whip crack, and then Almira Ann's wagon started to move.

"You get out of here, now," Sarah told Chatworth. "Can't you see that you're really and truly scaring Almira Ann?"

"I can't," Chatworth said. "The wagon is moving. But I'll get her unscared." He started to make little spider fingers over the squares of the quilt and up Almira Ann's arm. She pushed his hand away, but a bit of a smile peeked out.

"I'm a big spider," Chatworth crooned in the same voice Mama used when she played with him when he was a baby. "Coming to get you."

It was so silly that Sarah laughed, even though she didn't want to. Almira Ann laughed, too—and played along. "You can't get me." She scooched away from Chatworth's fingers and stood up.

Almira Ann and Chatworth were suddenly full of fun, jostling back and forth. Almira Ann was shrieking with laughter. All Sarah wanted to do was get in the game. Or was that lump of a feeling in the middle of her chest envy again?

Whatever it was, Sarah knew what to do. She pulled the quilt very quietly over her head. She waited for the next pause in Almira Ann's laughter. Then, in the instant of silence, she flung the quilt off her head and let out her most bloodcurdling wail.

Almira Ann screamed and leaped back. Sarah felt frozen to the floor. She flung out her arms as Almira Ann groped in the air for a moment and then tumbled backward out of the wagon.

Terrible Trouble

"Stop!" Sarah yelled to Almira Ann's pa. "Stop the oxen!" She climbed out onto the tongue and jumped down.

Almira Ann groaned. She was lying on the ground. "The wagon wheel rolled over my leg," she whispered as Sarah bent over her. Almira Ann's pa rushed up.

"Sarah," Chatworth called from the wagon. "The goat. Get the goat."

Sarah whirled around. Queen Victoria was disappearing inside a goat's mouth. *"Wah!"* Sarah hit the goat on the nose and tugged. Queen Victoria's head came off in her hand. She held on to it and ran. All up the line, the wagons were stopping.

"Mercy!" Grandmother said when Sarah raced up to the wagon.

"Hurry," Sarah panted. She tugged on Papa's arm. "You all have to go to Almira Ann's wagon. Take the medicine bag," she said to Mama.

After they had rushed off, she crawled inside the wagon and stuffed Queen Victoria's head into the bag where she kept her things. She stuffed the beads in after. She didn't even want to look at them. Her throat hurt. She couldn't bear to think about what might be happening with Almira Ann.

After a while Mama found Sarah and stroked her hair. "I'm sure Almira Ann knows you didn't mean to hurt her," Mama said.

"Is the leg broke?" Sarah heard Papa ask.

"It's broken pretty badly," Mama whispered. "We tried to set it with a splint and bandage, but it needs more support."

"Maybe we can find a doctor at Fort Laramie," Papa said.

A hot stuffiness filled Sarah's head. She wanted to fling herself into Mama's arms and wail like a baby, but she couldn't. She couldn't do anything but lie limp.

That whole day, Sarah felt like a crumpled-up rag doll. It was hard to walk when all she wanted to do was cry. After the wagons stopped at noon, she sat staring at Almira Ann's wagon while Grandmother and Mama made bread. What could she do to help Almira Ann?

Early in the evening Mama herself began to wail. Sarah was walking behind the wagon, patting Clovercup, when she heard it. She rushed toward the sound.

"What is it?" she heard Papa say. He took Mama's face in his hands.

"My wedding ring," Mama cried. "I took it off to mix the dough and hung it on a branch."

"Where we nooned, you mean?"

"Can't we go back?" Sarah asked Papa. "Can't

we please turn around and go back?" She knew they couldn't, though. They'd been on the road for hours since noon. And the captain, who was a bighearted man, was walking around urging everyone to push the oxen to get Almira Ann to Fort Laramie.

The next few days were awful. Mama didn't walk ahead and laugh with the others. She walked beside the oxen with her head down. Sarah saw both Papa and Grandmother looking at Mama with worried looks.

Sarah's stomach was one big knot of worry. Would Mama stay sad forever? Was Almira Ann in terrible pain? She must be missing Queen Victoria frightfully much.

When they nooned by a deep spring, Sarah found Chatworth pretending to fish, imitating the older boys, and grabbed his collar. "Here," she said. "I just filled this bucket with sweet water. You need to take it to Almira Ann's wagon."

He made a face at her. "You do it. I'm fishing."

"Please, Chatworth." She wanted to shake him, but she made herself be calm. "No one wants to see me there. I'm sure they hate me."

He still shook his head until she gave him a hard look and said fiercely, "Almira Ann's fall was partly your fault, too, Chatworth."

He looked at his feet and mumbled something, but he picked up the bucket. Sarah sighed. Now she had made Chatworth feel bad, too.

Later, when she saw him swinging the empty bucket, she rushed over. "How is she?"

"She moans a lot," Chatworth said. He looked pale and pulled away from Sarah's hand. Sarah felt wretched. If only there really were some way for Almira Ann to ride to Oregon inside an egg.

She couldn't bear to walk with people she knew—people she'd let down—so she spent the day falling in with this group and that. That's how she learned that they would be at Fort Laramie by night. She heard other names, too—Rocky Ridge, Soda Springs. She felt like a sharp, rocky ridge herself.

As she listened to a group of women, she found out that Papa had come up with an idea for Almira Ann's leg. The women were sure it wouldn't work. One of the women called Papa "dreamer" again.

When they finally got to Fort Laramie, Sarah turned in a slow circle, looking at everything. For miles and miles around Fort Laramie, the land was flat. Far away, Sarah could see mountains with snow on their tips. Only a third of the trip was over, the guidebook said. How would they ever make it through such mountains? And would Almira Ann have to stay in Fort Laramie?

After a while, Grandmother said, "Come along. You can help me with the shopping."

"Have you heard whether they found a doctor here?" Sarah asked.

"No." Grandmother's face was softer for a minute. "I don't believe they found a doctor."

Grandmother clucked and fussed over the prices. Sarah tried to help, but she kept hearing people talking—talking about Almira Ann. "She'll

never make it now," someone said. What did that mean?

"Do you think Almira Ann will have to give up going to Oregon?" she asked Papa when they got back to the wagon.

"I've been thinking about a plan," Papa said slowly. "I'm not sure it will work. But I'm going to try."

The next day, while the oxen rested, Papa worked on his plan. Sarah helped Grandmother wash clothes. All the while, she wondered what was happening.

"It's done!" Papa said with excitement at suppertime. "The carpenter shop had some pine planks I could use. Now the broken leg is all snug in a pine box! The box will hold it firm until it has a chance to heal."

Mama looked up. She looked interested in something for the first time since she lost her ring. "That poor child," she said. "How wonderful that you were able to help."

Papa bent over her tenderly. "And look what I bought for us at the store." Sarah laughed as she saw what Papa, in his very Papa way, had hoped would cheer Mama up—a bottle of lemon syrup, a can of preserved quinces, and some raisins.

She felt a giant relief that Almira Ann would get to go on to Oregon. At the same time, she couldn't imagine anything more wretched. Poor Almira Ann, bouncing along in a wagon with her leg in a pine box.

Perhaps the goodies that Papa brought did cheer Mama up. The next morning, Sarah heard her singing again. "Come with me," she said when Sarah poked her head out of the tent. "I want to check on Mrs. Tinker."

"The lady who was sick?"

"Not sick, exactly."

As they got close to Mrs. Tinker's wagon, Sarah was amazed to hear a tiny wail. Inside, Mrs. Tinker held the baby up in its blanket for Mama and Sarah to see. "Her name is California," she told them. "That's where my husband is determined to go."

Sarah stared down at little California, sucking her fingers. She couldn't help but smile.

Mama touched Sarah's cheek softly. "It's good to see you smile."

When they left the wagon, Mama said, "It pained me to lose my ring. But it pained me more to see my daughter's hurt and know I had nothing in my medicine bag to help that kind of hurt."

"Do you have anything in your medicine bag to help Almira Ann?"

"I have comfrey," Mama said. "I'll make a poultice and take it there."

Sarah hesitated. "Will you see if Almira Ann wants me to visit her?"

When Sarah saw Mama coming back, she ran to her.

"Almira Ann is feeling very low," Mama said gently. "I don't believe you should visit just yet." Sarah felt such a heavy sadness weighing her down, she could hardly walk.

Nothing cheered her up—not seeing buffalo, with their huge, shaggy heads. Not camping beside the Sweetwater, with its clear, cold water.

Not even Independence Rock. While other people painted or carved their names, Sarah just sat with her head leaning against Clovercup. She'd had enough of names on rocks. How far away Independence, Missouri, felt from Independence Rock, not quite Oregon Territory.

Once they left Independence Rock, everyone seemed worn out and weary. "Now we begin to climb the Rocky Mountains in earnest," Grandmother said. Sarah patted Clovercup, hoping she would be strong enough to climb a mountain.

By the time they reached the Parting of the Ways, people's weary spirits burst into bitter arguments. "If we take the cutoff, we'll save fifty to seventy-five miles," the captain told everyone. "But we won't find a drop of water or a bit of grass between the Big Sandy and the Green River."

Sarah shivered as she watched the men vote. Everyone's eyes already itched and burned from the dust. Would the desert between the Big Sandy and the Green River be much worse?

Secret Plan

Sarah's sunbonnet didn't seem to keep the sun out even one little bit. The sun seemed to be reaching down to smack her on the head. Her spirit had never felt so shriveled and small.

The dust was a powder that burned into the skin. When Chatworth slogged by, she saw that his cheeks were peeling. "Are you all right?" she called to him. Her voice was hoarse.

"The animals and I are famishing for water," he croaked. Sarah noticed that his lip was split. She wished she could take back the sharp words she'd said to him. Grandmother was right.

Sarah's mind made a chant to go with her footsteps. "You're un-re-li-able. You're un-re-li-able."

She tried to think of something she could do to make amends. After all, you couldn't just say "I'm sorry" when you did something like she'd done to Almira Ann. If only she could think of some way to show how really, really sorry she was.

By afternoon, some oxen were stumbling. People began to throw out their heavy things, trying to make the loads easier for the animals to pull. Sarah saw a man standing beside a pair of weak-looking oxen, staring at a huge rolling pin in his hands. "Oh, the biscuits my dear mother used to make with this," he said sadly as he put it down on the ground.

Trunks and tables sat by the trail—and some huge oak drawers that someone must have hoped would hold clothes in Oregon. Now the oak was scuffed and cracked. The desert wind danced and howled around people's beloved things.

Sarah was glad Papa had taken such good care of their oxen that they still looked strong.

"Ready to unload the table?" she heard Papa ask Grandmother. Even in the heat, his voice still had a smile in it.

"Not my table." Sarah thought Grandmother would hold the oxen up herself if she had to.

"So far, our team still seems strong," Papa said. "Let's keep the table a little longer."

When darkness dropped that evening, a cold wind came up. Better, Sarah thought. But the thirst was still everywhere. And the wagons showed no signs of stopping. Papa came up behind her. "I'm going to untie Clovercup," he said. "Try milking her. That way you children will have a bit to drink."

"Are we going to stop?" Sarah asked.

"Maybe for an hour or two. Mostly we need to get to water. If we can."

Poor Clovercup didn't seem to want to give much milk. "That's all right," Sarah said, patting her. "You did the best you could."

She stood, looking down at the pail. The milk danced there, pale and a little fuzzy. She blinked to clear her eyes. It wouldn't hurt to drink a lit-

tle of it. Just a tiny bit. She dipped the cup in the pail. She lifted it to her dry lips. Then she shook her head. No, not one sip. The least she could do was give the milk to Chatworth.

On the afternoon of the second desert day, the exhausted oxen smelled the water first. They tossed their heads and snorted. Sarah stared ahead. At first, she saw nothing. Then she thought her eyes must be crazy from the dazzle of shiny dried lakes. But Papa appeared out of the shimmering sand, sweat and dirt smeared on his face, and called, "The Green River."

"Thank God," Mama breathed. She grabbed Chatworth's hand.

Before long, the oxen stumbled into a clumsy gallop. "Come on!" Papa yelled. Even Clover-cup managed a slow trot.

Sarah let her go. Her throat was full of dust as she watched the wagons lurch by. When they were all past, she started walking again. Maybe she would never catch up. Maybe she'd never see any of them again. It would serve her right.

But when she came up over a rise, there was the river—and there everyone was, laughing and throwing water, standing in the river. Chatworth was pouring water over his head, giggling.

All except for Almira Ann, of course. Grandmother was right, Sarah thought. Envy had robbed her of everything dear.

Finally Sarah walked down for a long drink and ducked her whole head in the cool water. Then she sat under a tree, smelling the fresh sweetness of its leaves—still mixed with the smell of dust. "Come in," Chatworth called.

Sarah shook her head. She took off her dripping sunbonnet, put it in her lap, and sat, watching.

That night, she stirred the beans and molasses in the iron pot hanging over the fire while Mama and Grandmother rinsed clothes in the river. Her eyes felt on fire from the dust, and when the smoke got in them, it felt good to cry.

After a while, Grandmother told Chatworth to spread the rubber cloth on the ground and put the tin plates on top. "Supper," she called to Papa, who was mending the oxen's yoke.

Papa settled himself on the ground. "They say we're halfway to Oregon," he said. For a moment, he was quiet. Then his tired eyes suddenly had their old sparkle. "And when we get there, we'll see . . ."

"Fat pigs already cooked, running around with knives and forks in them," Chatworth and Papa said together.

Grandmother smoothed her skirt. "I, for one, will be glad to eat those pigs seated at my own dining table."

After the beans were gone, Mama handed out dried apple slices. Chatworth flung his on the rubber cloth. "Better eat it," Grandmother warned. "We have a ways to go. You could still get scurvy."

All at once Mama said, "We have a special day coming soon. Then we'll have lemon syrup."

Sarah saw Papa smile at Mama.

"And pickles?" Chatworth asked.

"And pickles."

Chatworth ran off. Sarah chewed on her apple slice. A few minutes later, Chatworth came tearing back. "A wagon . . . ," he panted. "The oxen just tipped a wagon down the bank and broke a wheel all to smash. Captain says we'll have to hold here and find wood to fix it."

"Whose wagon?" Grandmother asked.

Chatworth didn't look at Sarah. "Almira Ann's," he said in a low voice.

Sarah leaped to her feet. But then she didn't know what to do next. "Mercy!" Mama said. "Was Almira Ann hurt?"

"Someone said she wasn't."

Papa started off toward the river. "Wait," Grandmother called to him. "Tell them they must take my dining table. It will have plenty of wood to fix the wheel."

"But Grandmother," Chatworth said. "What will you eat your pig on, then?"

Grandmother didn't hesitate. "I'd eat on the ground rather than see our old neighbors suffer."

Sarah stared into the fire, where it cracked and hissed. Somewhere across the camp, she heard the sad whisper of a flute. "Worse and worse," she said to herself. "Worse and worse and worse."

Not traveling the next morning felt funny. Sarah helped make johnnycake for breakfast. Chatworth ran up and pinched a bit of cornmeal. "Why can't we have a real cake?" he asked.

Mama just shook her head. Then, as Chatworth was about to run off, Mama suddenly took his arm and whispered to him. Sarah heard the words "special day" and "seven days." Sarah could guess what she was talking about. But she could hardly bear to think about the special day. "Are you going to take comfrey to Almira Ann again today?" she asked Mama.

Mama nodded. "Papa said Almira Ann asked about you last night," she said gently. "I believe you may soon have a chance to try to make amends."

After breakfast was cleaned up, Sarah climbed to the top of the rise. She could see Almira Ann's wagon with the men gathered around it, working on the wheel. She stared down at Almira Ann's wagon. Sometimes, as Mama said, seeing someone else's hurt was worse than feeling your own. It was worse when you had caused that hurt. What could she possibly do to make amends?

A movement caught her eye. Mrs. Tinker climbing out of her wagon. Was this baby California's first time to see the sky? Suddenly Sarah had a thought. Mama had taken Sarah to see California Tinker to cheer up her spirit. Was there anything she could do to cheer up Almira Ann?

Maybe she could take California Tinker over there. She imagined Almira Ann's face looking down at the baby. No! Of course! She knew what would help even more. Sarah began to trot down the hill, making her plan as she went.

Next morning, the camp stirred at four. Sarah milked Clovercup and hung the pail under the wagon. One by one, the wagons began to turn into the long line. Sarah helped Chatworth into the wagon and climbed up after him. Papa always made them ride inside when they were crossing a river.

As they jounced down the bank, Sarah closed her eyes. How did Almira Ann bear it?

When she opened her eyes again, river swirled around the wagon. "I know a secret," Chatworth said. "Your birthday is in less than a week."

"I know."

"Almira Ann's birthday, too," Chatworth said.

"Something else, too," Sarah said. For the first time in a long while, she felt a little like smiling.

"America's birthday," they said together. Chatworth laughed.

They nooned in the shade that day. "It's good to see wood again," Grandmother said. Sarah got the pail from under the wagon.

After their bread and butter, she and Chatworth were supposed to rest. The shade was as cool as the smooth buttermilk, but Sarah was restless. She inched on her stomach until she was close to where Mama, Papa, and Grandmother were talking.

". . . upset for so long," she heard Mama say. She inched a bit closer. Were they talking about her?

"Perhaps she'll cheer up for her birthday," Papa said. "She'll see a sight for it, that's for sure. Soda Springs."

Sarah listened as he talked on, telling Mama and Grandmother what the guidebooks said about Soda Springs. An excited spirit rippled through her as she listened. Yes! Here was something else she could do.

The Most Glorious Present

Even with Mama's help, the first part of the plan was very hard. Sometimes Sarah thought she would die of frustration, sitting in the wagon, making her fingers do the careful work. But then she thought of Almira Ann bumping along in her own wagon. It made her determined to succeed.

Finally, the night before her birthday, long after she was supposed to be asleep, she crept out of the tent and found her way to where Papa, Mama, and Grandmother sat by the fire. She took a deep breath. "Can I have anything I want for my birthday?" she asked.

Grandmother gave one of her sniffs. "Goodness, no," she said, right away.

"What I would like," Sarah went on quickly, "is . . . is the bottle of lemon syrup that Papa got at Fort Laramie."

Mama looked at her in surprise. "Whatever would you want lemon syrup for?"

Sarah tried to think about how she would explain her plan. She wasn't even sure it would work. Would it sound foolish, the way Papa's plans sounded to people?

Suddenly Grandmother spoke again. "Heavens, what's the harm?" she said. "Let the child have what she wants."

Sarah stared at Grandmother. She couldn't see Grandmother's face well by the firelight. But when Grandmother talked that way, the matter was settled.

The next morning before breakfast, Mama handed the bottle to Sarah without a word. "I thought it was for our special celebration," Chatworth said.

Mama hushed him. "We'll think of something else special."

"Pickles?"

"Probably pickles."

Sarah crawled up into the wagon and put the syrup in her bag with the project she'd been working on. Everything had to stay safe until Soda Springs. She jumped down, wondering if her plan was really going to work.

A bit after noon, she saw that Grandmother was walking a little way ahead. Sarah hurried to catch up. "Thank you, Grandmother," she panted. "I really, really wanted the lemon syrup."

Grandmother was quiet. Sarah waited for some kind of lecture. But when Grandmother spoke, all she said was, "I know you have been carrying a heavy load of sadness about what happened to Almira Ann."

Grandmother's unexpected kindness made Sarah feel like crying. "Do you think Almira Ann will ever forgive me?" she whispered.

"We can't worry about that, child." Grandmother's voice had some of its old tartness back.

"When we wrong someone, we must simply do the right thing and trust that that is that."

Then her voice softened again. "Sarah," she said, "we have a long trip ahead of us yet. I've heard people talk about the steep Blue Mountains and the Cascade Mountains. I know the hardships in front of us."

Sarah sighed. It would be double hard for Almira Ann. Maybe she and Chatworth could figure out ways to help Almira Ann's parents with their work.

"Once," Grandmother went on, "I would have said this family could never make it. I believe I even said something like that to you."

"Yes," Sarah said. "I keep thinking that you might be right."

"But I don't think I was right," Grandmother said. "I see I didn't give anyone enough credit. Your father is a dreamer—but his dreams have brought plans that nobody else thought of."

Sarah reached out shyly and took Grandmother's hand. Grandmother's skin was rough and cracked, but her voice was gentle as she went on. "I always thought your mother was frivolous. But when she was sad after she lost her ring, I felt as if a light had gone out. Now I know that your mother's joyous spirit gives me courage."

Suddenly, up ahead, they heard a shout. Coming up over the next rise, Sarah saw they had reached the place Papa had talked about. Water fizzed from the ground. People were running from spring to spring, tasting the water and shouting. While they watched, Chatworth stuffed his hat over the top of a cone that growled and hissed. A burst of water filled the hat and blew the top off. Chatworth laughed. Even Grandmother laughed.

It was true, Sarah thought, peeking at Grandmother. They all had surprises in them. She turned to run back to the wagon. But Grandmother squeezed Sarah's hand. "One more thing," Grandmother said. "When I watched you give Chatworth the milk that thirsty night, I saw that you make many mistakes, but you also never give up trying to make things right. If I ever find myself stuck, with a big log across the road, you are the person I would want most on the other end."

Sarah felt as tall as Chimney Rock.

"Well, work's waiting," Grandmother said. "They say the soda in the water will make a good bread."

Sarah hurried to the wagon. She was nervous about what Almira Ann would say. But she whispered Grandmother's words to herself. "When we wrong someone, we must simply do the right thing and trust that that is that."

She knelt by a spring where the water was milky white. She swished a careful pan full of the water. In the pan, the water bubbled and danced. Sarah poured the lemon syrup into the water. Then she carefully carried the pan to Almira Ann's wagon.

Inside, the wagon was dim and hot and smelled of canvas, but Sarah could see Almira Ann with her leg in a box. She looked pale and small.

Sarah caught her breath. She lifted the pot. "This is for you," she said. "Because I'm sorry and because it's our birthday, Almira Ann."

At first, Almira Ann didn't say anything. Suddenly she dipped a cup into the pot and then sipped a little lemon fizz. "Ooo," she giggled. "It tickles my nose."

Sarah grinned. "One more thing," she said. She held out the new Queen Victoria. Mama had helped her make a new body and a dress from quilt scraps. But Sarah herself had carefully decorated the dress with the beads. It wasn't perfect, Sarah knew. But she thought it looked pretty splendid.

She watched as Almira Ann touched the beads with her soft fingers. Then Almira Ann smiled. "Do you know something?" she said. "Sarah Eliza Benton, you have brought me the two best presents in the whole, whole world."

Sarah let out a huge, rolling sigh.

"Run get a cup and help me drink this lemonade," Almira Ann said. "We'll never have an Oregon Trail birthday present like this again."

That night, Papa helped Almira Ann's pa roll back the wagon cover. Sarah and Almira Ann sat together, looking up at the stars. Papa and Mama, Grandmother and Chatworth, and Almira Ann's pa and mother gathered around the wagon, waiting for the fireworks. Mama had stewed up the last of the dried strawberries into dumplings. Everyone said "ah" over them. "Light as a cork," said Almira Ann's pa.

"I made lots of rag dolls while I was sitting here," Almira Ann said to Sarah. "You can pick as many as you want."

Sarah looked at her fingers. Sewing would never be her favorite thing. But she no longer felt envious. She could sew if she had to. "Will you show me how to make a rag doll, too?" Sarah asked.

"Of course."

"Then I can sit with you and make them," Sarah said. She made a silent vow that she would also collect jokes for Almira Ann—and treasures and stories and songs because they still had the Blue Mountains to go over. And Cascade Mountains. And probably some other hard things she didn't even know about. "Whatever happens," she told Almira Ann, "we'll all be right here with you."

"I've been thinking about my doll," Almira Ann said. "She doesn't look much like Queen Victoria anymore."

"I know," Sarah said sadly.

"It's all right, though," Almira Ann said. "She belongs to the Oregon Trail now. My father says we're following the footsteps of Lewis and Clark, so maybe I can call my doll Sacajawea."

Sarah stared up at the stars. Everything was changing. Who knew what they would look like or how their new homes would turn out when they finally got to Oregon? At least the adventure was grand.

The first of the fireworks fizzed into the air. It would never make it to the stars, Sarah thought. But what a glorious start to a journey.

AUTHOR'S NOTE

When Almira Ann and Sarah reached Soda Springs, they still had a long trip ahead of them. About fifty miles later, those immigrants who had decided to go to California split off and headed south and west. The Hastings and Benton families turned north. They had to travel about 300 miles along the rocky Snake River (where they had to climb down cliffs and back up just to have water to drink), over the steep Blue Mountains, and about 250 miles over the Cascade Mountains and down into the Willamette Valley. They didn't reach Oregon until almost Christmas.

Almira Ann and Sarah are fictional characters, but almost everything that happened to them in this book did happen to real children on the Oregon Trail. There was a girl, for instance, who rode all the way to Oregon with her leg in a pine box, and a mother who cut out animal-shaped cookies for a trail treat. Believe it or not, there was a girl whose cow fell into a gully and was eventually saved by boring holes in its horns. Many children gathered buffalo chips, dried buffalo droppings, to burn in place of firewood. And comfrey, an herb also called "knitbone," was useful in healing broken bones.

Traveling the Oregon Trail was not the same experience for everyone who made the trip. The wagons that traveled the trail had no springs—and most wagons had hardly any room inside because they were crammed with belongings the emigrants would need during the trip and afterward—so people walked whenever they could. Some people found the four- to six-month trip grueling or even tragic. But the early pioneers tended to come from farms and were used to working outside. A woman who made the trip in the 1850s described it as "easy and interesting." Another said that for her the "suffering" she'd heard about was merely "a little inconvenience" and that the pleasure overbalanced the hardship. Still another wrote in her journal that the other women walking ahead of the wagons were a "laughing, merry group."

The people the pioneers called "Sioux" called themselves the Lakota. While many of the pioneer journals talk about fear of the Native Americans, a woman who traveled the trail at age eleven later remembered, "Indians were a constant source of wonder and delight to me." Until the 1860s, hostile encounters with Native Americans were rare. Trades, such as the one in this book, were common.

Finally, one man who climbed Chimney Rock wrote in his journal that he found female names "as high as any on record" and was amazed that someone wearing skirts could have climbed to "a height so giddy."

My father was raised in eastern Oregon, and his family farmed over the ruts of the Oregon Trail. Dad and his brothers well remember riding in a wagon that would bounce and knock them off every time they went over one of the ruts. I myself was born in Portland, Oregon. Even though my parents moved to Ethiopia when I was only two years old and I spent almost all of my childhood there, Oregon was one of the few places I felt an attachment to in the United States. Two different years, we visited my grandparents on their farm in eastern Oregon and had exciting times, including games with the cousins and lots of doughnuts.

Much later, when I was living in Trinidad, Colorado, on the Santa Fe Trail, I became fascinated with trails. That's when I began to first read everything I could about the Oregon Trail. In 1990, I wrote an activity book, *The Oregon Trail: Dangers and Dreams,* that was sold in museums and gift shops along the trail. Even after years of reading and writing about traveling on the Oregon Trail, I've never become tired of thinking about what that journey must have been like for the families that left their homes (as my family did when I was young) and headed for a completely different country.

ACKNOWLEDGMENT

I would like to thank the many people who helped with this project, especially Cynthia Leitich Smith, who discussed a number of Native American issues with me and helped me choose which variant of Sacajawea's name would most probably be accurate for Almira Ann's time and place; my husband, Leonard, who took care of the family while I was traveling the trails; the Oregon California Trails Association, who taught me so much and who replaced valuable research materials destroyed in the 1997 Grand Forks flood; and the Kurtz storytellers for the tale of my great-great-grandmother's wedding ring.